Postcards to Herself

A Prose Poetry Novella

Laura Stamps

Postcards to Herself: A Prose Poetry Novella

ISBN: 978-1-962374-37-8 Paperback

ISBN: 978-1-962374-38-5 EPub

Library of Congress Control Number: 2025900736

Permissions have been granted and filed by the publisher.

Publisher: Prolific Pulse Press LLC

Prolificpulse.com admin@prolificpulse.com

Author Contact: laurastampsfiction.blogspot.com

Published March 2025 Raleigh, North Carolina USA

Table of Contents

Acknowledgements

Grateful acknowledgement is made to the following literary magazines and journals in which chapters from this novella first appeared: *Medusa's Kitchen, Anti-Heroin Chic, SPREAD, Little Old Lady Comedy, Cacti Fur, Indian Periodical, Northern Stars Magazine, Amethyst Review, Lothlorien Poetry Journal, The Gorko Gazette, The Beatnik Cowboy, The Rye Whiskey Review, Literary Yard, Synchronized Chaos, Impspired, Dark Winter Literary Magazine, Lone Stars Magazine, Academy of Heart and Mind, Erato Magazine, The Poet's Art, The Piker Press, Ancient City Poets.*

"Red Wagon" won an Honorable Mention Award in the *Northern Stars Magazine Poetry Competition.*

1. Postcards to Herself

Postcards. Elaine loves them. Yet nobody sends them. Not anymore. But why? A pretty postcard. In the mailbox. Scribbled with a tiny message. Personal. Intimate. Such fun to receive. I mean, what's not to like? What? Postcards. She decides to buy some. Fifty or so. Stores them in a decorative box. And then, and then. She contacts her friends. Asks if they'd like to send postcards. To each other. Would they? Will they? No. They'd rather text. They say. It's easier. Faster. They say. And it is. But then, but then. There was one friend. A poet. He loved postcards too. For years they sent postcards to each other. Just for fun. Handmade postcards. His. With fragments of his poems. She loved them. All of them. But he died. Postcards. She should send some. To herself. Just for fun. She reaches into the box. Selects one. "Dear Elaine," she writes to herself. "Bet you're surprised to hear from me. Me too."

2. To Elaine (With Love)

His postcards. Her poet friend. Bizarre works of art. That's what they were. But she loved them. All of them. Postcards. His. Cardboard cut with scissors. Decorated with images torn from magazines. Attached with Elmer's Glue. Wild collages. Crazy art. Crazy. Just like him. And she loved it. All of it. On the back he scribbled fragments of his poems. Or messages in Latin. A language she also knew. From high school. Two years of Latin. Another two in college. Four years of Latin. For her. But then, but then. That was thirty years ago. And now. He was still fluent. He was. In Latin. But she wasn't. Thank goodness for the Latin dictionaries. At Waldenbooks. The little paperbacks. She bought one. Just for his postcards. But she never told him. (Of course.) Postcards. Between friends. Some things are best left unsaid.

3. Seeds

She selects a postcard. A big one. From her box of postcards. She must have a hundred by now. Postcards. At least. "Dear Elaine," she writes to herself. "The flowers in my garden are troopers. They've survived four days of frost. And one hard freeze. Tough little critters. Those flowers. They are. Tougher than me. Much. This week I've been reading a book. By Thich Nhat Hanh. Angry people plant seeds in your soul. This he says. Anger, despair, deep sadness. The words they speak. They're seeds. Planting, planting. Seeds we water. When we believe them. Respond to them. Defend ourselves against them. Angry words. Watering, watering. Those seeds. They're in my soul. I can feel them. Seeds growing into weeds. Anger, despair, deep sadness. Weed seed. Inside me. I can feel it. Don't want it. It's not mine. Didn't come from me. But there it is. Seed planted. By angry people. And weeds. Too many. Rip them out. That's what I want. All of them. Gone. Like the weeds in my garden. But how? Maybe, maybe. Thich will tell me. In the meantime. What have you been up to? Can't wait to hear. Tell me, tell me. What say you?"

4. Red Wagon

In the mailbox today. Another postcard. Oh, this is fun! Writing postcards to herself. Mailing them. Receiving one or two every week. These postcards. And the messages they contain. Her dreams. Ideas. Observations. What she wants. What she's thinking about. What she wants to remember. Anything. Everything. Yes. This mail. These postcards. They make her smile. Just seeing one. Yes. They do that for her. And it doesn't matter. That she's the sender. That she's the receiver. Doesn't matter. None of it. None. She reaches into the decorative box on her desk. Selects a blank postcard. "Dear Elaine," she writes to herself. "Don't forget this. Don't. This image. I want to remember this. What I saw today. A chilly morning. Driving to work. And there. A young man. Maybe sixteen or so. On the sidewalk. Pulling a red wagon. Like a child's wagon. His cargo? Three tiny Chihuahuas. Bundled in warm sweaters. Sitting quietly. Serenely. In their red wagon. Enjoying the ride. The bright sunshine. The blue sky. The chilly air. And this young man. Out for a morning walk with his dogs. This image. It makes me smile. Just thinking about it. The four of them. Yes. There is still joy. Here. To be found. In this world. Plenty. Don't forget this. Don't. This image. There is joy."

5. Yellow

Another day. Another postcard. So much to say. "Dear Elaine," she writes. "The leaves are changing. I can't stop them. I wish I could. But can't. Red, orange, brown, yellow. I don't like it. Just. Don't. Changing leaves. It means cold weather is coming. Winter. Coming, coming. And I'm not a fan. Not. Wish it would stay warm all year. Summer. Forever. I wish. But this. Reality. That's what this is. And change. Inevitable. I know, I know. By now. I should be good with this. Change. And reality. But I'm not. So there. A woman called the other day. She sounded like a robot. She wasn't. But she sounded like one. Some insurance program. Something I didn't need. That's what she was selling. Like a robot. In a bad mood. Reading her script. No thanks. That's what I told her. She didn't like me much after that. I could tell. And yet, and yet. There are so many reasons for joy. And happiness. In the present moment. In the here. In the now. Do robots know this? I wonder. There's a bush. Outside my window. Full of yellow leaves. Tiny leaves. In the afternoon when the sun hits it. Just right. Those leaves. Sizzle. Like a thousand spotlights. Glorious. They are. Even though I've never liked autumn. Or the color yellow. Especially yellow.

This tree. Those leaves. They could change my mind. Not about autumn. No. But yellow. Yes. I'll give them that. Okay. Enough about me. What's new with you? Tell me." Another day, another postcard. Finished. She addresses it. Adds a stamp. And mails it. To herself.

6. Holly

She sits down. At her desk. And selects a postcard. "Dear Elaine," she writes. "I used to be married. Loneliest years of my life. They were. My husband thought if he read my posts. Online. On Instagram. That was all he needed to know. About me. My life. That he never needed to listen to me. Discuss anything with me. Plan with me. Talk to me. Not that he didn't talk. He did. About himself. Endlessly. His worries. His problems. His complaints. His plans. Him. But here's the thing. Instagram is not my life. A snapshot. A glimpse. That's all it is. Too bad. He never knew that. Never realized I'm more than that. More than a post on Instagram. More. Much. Much. More. Too bad. So I left him. And then, and then. Six months later. I saw a dog. A Yorkie. Her photo. On a dog rescue page. Holly. That was her name. This Yorkie. Sweet, calm, affectionate, low energy. That's how the rescue described her. Ten years old. A senior with a skin condition. That too. But those eyes. That face. I couldn't resist. Couldn't. Drove four hours to meet her. Adopted her. That day. Took her to a wonderful groomer. For a super short cut. Bought special food. To heal her itchy skin. Bought her warm sweaters. Lots of them. I did. Because, because. She was mine. And now.

We talk. Have wonderful discussions. Just the two of us. Holly and me. And now. She knows everything about me. All of it. All. Because she cares. Listens to me. Loves me. Hey. Forget Instagram. Forget it. Sometimes a dog is better than a husband. I mean, who knows, right? Well. I do. I know. Yeah, I do."

7. No Regrets

Saturday morning. Writing another postcard. She looks out the window. Oh. Geez. Not again. "Dear Elaine," she writes. "There's a tree. Next to the driveway. Fluffy. This tree. With a million leaves. At least. Maybe more. Probably. More. In the spring it coats my car with pollen. Greasy. Nasty stuff. In the summer it pelts my car with berries. Red. Juicy. Staining. And now, and now. In the fall. Those leaves. Zillions of them. Yes. There are. Falling on my car. Covering it. Glued to it. Every morning. Geez. What a mess. Okay. Moving on. To other news. There was a special program. On Netflix. Last night. This guru. Or something. I don't know. He said life is just a series of experiences. Nothing more. That's why we're here. On earth. To have experiences. As many as we need. One after another. No judgement. No regrets. Just experiences. Weird theory. I know. But on the plus side. Think about it. All the things I regret. You know. My stupid decisions. Wrong turns. Failed love relationships. All that stuff. Gone. Because, because. They'd just be experiences. Nothing more. No judgement. No regrets. Hey. Works for me. Totally. But still. There's this tree. Just another bad experience. For me. This tree. I don't need it. And those leaves. Zillions of them. Falling, falling. I wish my landlord would cut it down. Goodbye tree. Yeah. I could get into that. How nice. So nice. That would be."

8. Small

"Dear Elaine," she writes. "Today. This. This is what I'm thinking. Small. What's wrong with small? Bigger is better. That's what they say. But why? Huge. Famous. Notorious. Splashy. Slick. Slicker. Bells and whistles. All of them. More. More and more. But where does it end? Where? I'd rather be small. I think. The small things. In life. That's what matters to me. A smile. A hug. A kind word. It's enough. Isn't it? Yes? Yes. That's what I'm thinking. Today. Right now. Sitting in my small apartment. Writing this small letter. On a small postcard. Petting my small dog. I mean. I'm happy. My dog is happy. Small. What's wrong with that? Hey. You tell me."

9. Night Sky

"Dear Elaine," she writes on this postcard. "Sunday night. I was in bed. And through the curtains. I saw her. Venus. Bright in the sky. Like a headlight on high beam. Venus. This planet. Just seeing her made me happy. It did. No kidding. And then, and then. Last night. In bed. Again. Through the curtains. But she was gone. Venus. Vanished. Instead. There was a full moon. Huge. It was. So big it made me wonder. Is this one of those famous moons? You know. Blue Moon. Blood Moon. One of those. Again. Just seeing it there. In the night sky. It made me happy. (Geez. Am I easy to please, or what?) Of course. The big news this week isn't Venus or Blood Moons. No. It's a hurricane. The one rolling off the coast of Africa. The one that's coming our way. Or so they say. How crazy is that? I mean. It's November. It's cold outside. Weird, weird. I know. But even so. Tonight. This night. It's not about planets or hurricanes. No. Tonight. It's about Holly. My Yorkie. I promised her. This. That I'd search the web. For dental treats. To clean her teeth. You know. At Petco, PetSmart, Marshall's. Somewhere like that. Hey. Anything for Holly. My sweet doggie. But still, but still. In bed. Through the curtains. That sky. What will I see? Tonight. I wonder, wonder. What?"

10. Smile

Looking, looking. Through a box of postcards. Her collection. All these postcards. Must be a hundred by now. Maybe more. At least. And then she finds it. The one with the photo of a Yorkie. Yes. That's the one. That postcard. "Dear Elaine," she writes. "When I was meditating this morning. You know. Mindful breathing. Watching my breath. Concentrating on that. Inbreath, outbreath. Inbreath, outbreath. Like Thich Nhat Hanh teaches. I had a revelation. Thich would call it insight. I know. But it felt bigger than that. Bigger. Much, much. It was this. That I don't need anything. To be happy. That happiness can only be found in the present moment. Here. Now. No matter where I am. Anywhere. With anyone. Or without. I can be happy. In this moment. I mean. I used to think I needed something. You know. To be happy. That I needed to move to another city. To have more friends. To participate in more activities. Everything we're taught we need. To be happy. But that's not true. Happiness. It's already here. Now. In me. In this present moment. I don't need anything else. To be happy. None of us do. Imagine that? Light. So light. That's how I felt. And free. That too. Anyway. I thought I'd mention this. To give you a smile. If you haven't had one.

Today. If you're not smiling. Already. Like me. Right now. Smiling, smiling. Sorry. I can't stop."

11. Green

"Dear Elaine," she writes. "You'll never guess what happened. To me. Today. Driving down Tucker Road. To the post office. The traffic lights. You should have seen it. Every light was green. One right after the other. No kidding. I mean. You know how many there are. Seven or eight. Those traffic lights. And most are red. Always. They are. For me. But not today. Green. Every one of them. And all the way down. To the post office. Odd. Don't you think? I wonder, wonder. Is someone trying to tell me something? I mean. This never happens to me. Never. All those green lights. One right after the other. This is a sign. Isn't it? Has to be. Has to mean something. It does. I can feel it. There's a message in here somewhere. But what? What? Who knows? Although. When I think about it. Go, go, go. That's what green means. But where? Go where? Go shopping? Great idea! Shopping. Always good for the soul. It is. Shopping. But where? Where to go? Well, there's PetSmart. And all those doggie sweaters. In every size. Christmas sweaters. They've got them. Lots of them. I should get one. For Holly. A Christmas sweater. Green. Yorkie-size. Maybe two. Hey. That's it! Mystery solved. Green lights. Green doggie sweaters. Yeah. Sounds good to me. Okay.

Got to run. I'm off to PetSmart. With Holly. For a Christmas sweater. Maybe two. In the meantime, how are you?"

12. Some People

Saturday afternoon. Walking to the park. Elaine and Holly. Too many leaves today. It was the hurricane. Last week. That's what did it. Stripped half the leaves off the trees. The rest have taken flight today. Falling, falling. On streets, cars, sidewalks. Leaves. Everywhere. Swirling, swirling. One lands on Holly's back. A maple leaf. She ignores it. Continues walking toward the park. Her harness buckled over a Christmas sweater. Yorkie-size. Nice and warm. For a chilly day. Like today. A moped turns onto the street. Heads toward them. Elaine glances at it. Mopeds. Funny little machines. Men are the ones who seem to like them. Ride them. Mopeds. Not her thing. Yet there's something odd about this one. The rider's coat. It's not a jacket. Not the kind a man would wear. This coat. Too bulky. Furry. A fur coat. Leopard print. That's what it is. And the moped. Bright fuchsia. A woman on her moped. Imagine that? She speeds past Elaine in a whirl of autumn leaves. Just a flash of pink. And she's gone. Holly ignores it. Continues walking. Into the park. Walking, walking. Until she reaches a bench. Their bench. Elaine pulls a package of doggie bones from her pocket. Peanut butter. Holly's favorite. They sit on the bench. Together. Watching cars go by. Watching trees shed their leaves. And Elaine smiles. She can't help it. That leopard-print coat. That pink moped. Some people just know how to live.

13. Hail Mary

Looking, looking. For a postcard. In the box on her desk. So many pretty ones. These postcards. But, but, but. Which one? A palm tree. Yeah. That's the one. That's it. "Dear Elaine," she writes. "This week I can't seem to pray. Correctly. You know. My rosary. It's the Lord's Prayer. I keep messing it up. I do. But why? Not a clue. Maybe I need a new rosary. You think? Maybe then. I could get it right. I mean. I've prayed this prayer a zillion times. At least. A million. You know I have. So I'm thinking. What's wrong with me? Geez. Who knows? But this. This I do know. It's only November. And I'm already tired of the cold. Tired of winter. Done with it. I am. I should pack a bag. Grab Holly's doggie toys. A package of treats. Maybe two. And head for Florida. Pretend we're snowbirds. Maybe, maybe. Stop in St. Augustine. Yeah. Stay there awhile. In that city. The one named after a Catholic saint. I mean. How perfect is that? New rosary. New city. Maybe then. I could pray a decent rosary. Who knows? That might be all I need. Possibly. Maybe. I don't know. Do you? Could be, could be. What do you think?"

14. And Then There's This

She selects another postcard. An etching of a sunflower. Her favorite. Sunflowers. So pretty. She loves them. Really. She does. "Dear Elaine," she writes. "I was watching a YouTube video last night. A therapist. Possibly spiritual. Could have been. Can't remember. Anyway, he was talking about the benefits of the present moment. You know. Living your entire life in the present. Every day. All of it. Every minute. He said most of us never do that. Instead we live in the past or the future. Well, we do. It's true. You know it is. And he said this. This. If the past is created in the present moment. And it is. That means you have the power. All the power. To rewrite your past. And you can. Now. In the present moment. Makes sense. Doesn't it? I mean. We do it anyway. Every day. But we never think about it. And we should. You know. Just imagine. If you based every decision on creating a positive past. There'd be nothing to regret. No cringe-worthy memories. No bad decisions. Or stupid choices. Or bad-news relationships. All the things that you regret. That I regret. And I do. All of it. All the time. The things I wish I could go back and change. Now that I know better. Now that I'm thinking clearly. I am. I hope. Thinking clearly. Just imagine. Having nothing to regret. Radical. I know. This focus. This change. But a good thing. Something to consider. I mean. It's worth a try. Don't you think? Don't you?"

15. Yams

"Dear Elaine," she writes on a postcard to herself. "You'll never guess what I did yesterday. Went to the grocery store to buy four cans of yams. Came home with four cans of carrots. Didn't even realize it. Got home. Looked in the bag. No yams. Just carrots. What? What? Still don't know how that happened. My brain. Where was it? Geez. And this. While I'm writing this. This postcard. There's a spot on the window. And it's moving. No. Wait. Not a spot. A ladybug. That's what it is. Must be November. That's when the ladybugs hatch. The eaves of this apartment building are full of them. And centipedes. They're up there too. They hatch in the spring. I think. But don't quote me on that. And this. What's the deal with winter? Stingy, stingy with the sun. It is. So gray. Someone should teach it to share. The sun. Sunshine. I miss it. I do. But those carrots. Can you believe it? Where was my brain? Where? Oh, well. Carrots. I'll eat them. Every can. You know I will. As for my brain. I know, I know. Should be kinder to myself. I should. I mean. We all have our moments. Right? I guess. But then. I really did want those yams."

16. Pony Cars

A new day. A new postcard. "Dear Elaine," she writes. "Okay. First thing. These sirens. Outside my window. Sirens. More than one. Screaming, screaming. For 30 minutes now. No kidding. Continuous. They are. No break in their wail. And it makes me wonder, wonder. What is it? Maybe an accident? With a pony car? You know the ones. On Tucker Road. The cars that zoom up behind you. At 90 mph. At least. Maybe faster. Probably. Faster. I mean. Suddenly. There they are. Filling my rearview mirror. Like bad news. Like demons. That's what they are. Coming to devour my car. Or me. As I drive the speed limit. Always. On Tucker Road. And then, and then. They're gone. Racing past me. To fill the rearview mirror of someone else. To give them a chill. Or worse. And those sirens. Still wailing. So many. What's happening? I wonder, wonder. Who knows? But this I do know. Pony cars. Not my thing. Not me. No ponies for me. No. Not my car. Not with Holly. A pup car. That's my car. Holly next to me. Buckled in her doggie car seat. Singing. Yes, we do. Often. Driving the speed limit. Down Tucker Road. And those sirens. Still wailing. Outside my window. Screaming, screaming. But not for us."

17. Little

"Dear Elaine," she writes. "Saturday morning. Blue skies. Freezing temps. Bright sunshine. It's grocery shopping day. These little shopping carts. At Food Lion. Oh, how I love them! So easy to maneuver. Yes. Easy is good. Down one aisle. And then another. Apples, pears, bananas. Salad greens. Canned vegetables. Potato chips. All of that. I toss in my cart. And then, and then. I stop. At the pet food aisle. Dog treats. That's what I need. But look at them. Look! So many. Too many. No way to choose. Even if I linger, linger. To study them. To read each label. Even then. I can't decide. So I grab the prettiest package. And run. Thank goodness for Holly. Have mercy on me, I tell her. Have mercy. And she does. She eats them all. Every time. Such a good dog. She is. Yes. And little too. Like my shopping bags. The ones I bring from home. My little bags. Colorful. Decorative. Perfect for little shopping carts. The cashier rings up my groceries. And we chat. I know him. Nice guy. But then, but then. The lady behind me in line. She asks about my bags. Are they gift bags? No. They aren't. She thinks my little bags are weird. No. They aren't. But then, but then. She turns. To the man behind her. What does he think? About my bags. (Seriously?) Poor woman. Geez.

What can you say? Some people really need a
dog."

18. What Does It Take?

"Dear Elaine," she writes on another postcard. "I've been thinking, thinking. Today. About my ex-husband. You remember him. Right? The tall guy. Always in a hurry. Yeah. That was him. Couldn't walk with me like a normal person. No. He had to zoom ahead. Always. Like a rocket. On those long legs of his. And I'd have to yell at him. To get his attention. To make him stop. And then. He'd look surprised. Always. I mean. He never realized I wasn't there. Invisible. Evidently. That was me. Spent most of my marriage talking to the back of his head. Conversation. Not his thing. While I was talking. To him. Trying. He'd walk away. Said he thought I was finished. Oh, really? Too hyper. Him. To stand still. To listen. Even though he was chatty. Yeah. He was. Constantly. Mumbling. Mostly. Entire conversations. He'd have. With me. When I wasn't in the room. Important things. Things I needed to know. He'd say to an empty room. I'd hear a mumbling noise. Somewhere in the house. And I'd have to yell at him. To get his attention. To make him stop. Remind him. You know. That I'm not in the same room. Invisible. In our marriage. Evidently. That was me. So here's the thing. What does it take for a man to stop? To look you in the eye. Listen. Respond. With more than one word. Can men do that? A conversation. Two people. In the same room. Talking to each other. Back and forth. Give and take. Is that possible? For a man. Any man? Tell me. I'd like to know."

19. What Does It Mean?

Asleep. She is. Right now. Or halfway. Yeah. Probably. Half. Half asleep. But then, but then. There's a knock at the door. And a cardboard box. Somebody left it. On her door mat. A Chihuahua. Tan and white. Tiny, tiny. Six or seven pounds. In a pink harness. Sitting in the box. Looking up at her. Those eyes! Scared, confused, pleading. For what? What? Elaine leans down. There's a note taped to the box. Missy. That's her name. This little dog. Ten years old. Sweet, calm, potty-trained. (Or so the note says.) But it's not signed. This note. Instead. There's a request. To take care of her. Missy. Because, because. This person can't. Not anymore. Elaine looks at the dog. Surrounded by toys. A leash. A package of treats. But then, but then. The alarm goes off. Elaine opens her eyes. Oh. It was just a dream. That's all. A dream. And yet, and yet. You know?

20. Light

So many postcards. So much to say. "Dear Elaine," she writes to herself. "Almost Christmas. Can you tell? It's the reindeer. They're everywhere. Their antlers rising from car windows. Tiny Christmas trees. Those too. On these windows. These cars. Antlers and Christmas trees sprouting from the same window. Insane, I know. And wreaths. Can't forget those. Attached to hoods and trunks. And Christmas decals. Plastered on every door. It's too much. You know? Too, too much. So I'm thinking. When did a car become a Christmas decoration? I mean. Really. Is that crazy? Or what? But nothing beats what I saw today. Nothing. There. In front of the old bowling alley. You know the one. On Tucker Road. He was there. This man. Waiting for the bus. Wearing a suit and tie. Bright orange. That suit. And leopard print. I kid you not. Orange leopard print. From head to toe. Can you imagine? But that's not all. The lapels. On that suit. Orange fur. I'm serious. Fluffy, fluffy fur. All around his neck. So I'm thinking. Is this what a pimp looks like? I don't know. Never seen one before. But I'll tell you this. This man. This suit. The only bright spot. He was. On the street. Today. In dreary weather. Cloudy. Freezing cold. And yet, and yet. This beacon of light. Him. This man. This suit. I mean. Isn't that what we're called to be? A light. In a dark world. Or something like that. I mean. You do what you can with what you've got. Right? And he did. So I'm thinking. Mission accomplished. So there."

21. Sunburn

"Dear Elaine," she writes on a new postcard. "I used to drink in high school. I did. Not my fault. The drinking. It was JoBeth. She started it. Best friends in high school. Yes. We were. Went to Daytona Beach together. Our senior year. Spring break. I'll never forget it. Two days on the sand. Burned to a crisp. Lobsters. That would be us. JoBeth said bathing in milk was good. You know. For sunburn. Prevents peeling. Okay, then. Off to the 7-Eleven we went. JoBeth bought a carton of milk. And two beers. I bought a jar of Noxzema. (I'd heard it was better for sunburn.) In the car she gave me one of the beers. Said she bought it for me. I didn't drink. But we were eighteen. And legal. Okay, then. Why not? That first beer. Tasted like pond scum. (How could I be so stupid?) Three days later I was drinking like a pro. Tasted great. All of it. Beer. (Lots of that.) Drinks with tiny umbrellas. Wine spritzers. Margaritas. Anything. Everything. I tried it. Loved it. All of it. We flew home a week later. JoBeth looked like a tanned goddess. Not me. I was peeling like an orange. (Noxzema? Total fail.) A year later I stopped drinking. Started dating a drug dealer. (How could I be so stupid?) No brain cells back then. None. Obviously. I blame it all on the beer."

22. Bullet

She reaches into the box. And selects another postcard. "Dear Elaine," she writes. "It's January. And I rarely see the sun anymore. But when it appears. Sunshine. A sunny day. Like today. When I was driving home from work. I see people out walking. In this glorious sun. Men power-walking. Teenage girls. Gossiping, giggling. Families trying to keep up with each other. Women walking with strollers. And this. Just now. This. As I was driving home. This man. Wearing a frizzy wig. Or that's what it looked like. A wig. Lime green. With orange bangs. I kid you not. In a muscle shirt. He was. Pumping hand weights. I think. No. Actually. Prancing with weights. He was. But that hair. Geez. What if it wasn't a wig? I mean. Maybe it's his hair. Green. Like the Jell-O we had to eat as kids. My mother's favorite. The only kind she would buy. Green Jell-O. A fate worse than death. It was. And orange marmalade. That too. Her favorite. Not strawberry. Not grape. Nothing tasty like that. No. Just orange marmalade. Her favorite jelly. Again. A fate worse than death. Truly. It was. And yet, and yet. I guess. I should count my blessings. Right? Like the Benedictine monks. Living a life of gratitude. Grateful for everything. Okay. I can do that. I can be grateful. For my hair.

That it didn't turn green. From a childhood diet. Of lime green Jell-O. And my bangs. Thankful. That they're not orange. Like marmalade. So, so grateful. I am. To have dodged that family bullet. Me. Gratitude. Yeah. Living the life. I am."

23. Allergies

"Dear Elaine," she writes. "I have a co-worker at the gift shop. You know. Where I work. In the mall. Roxanne. That's her name. Anyway. She'd like to have a dog. But can't. Allergies. Bad ones. Really bad. So she emails photos to me. Dog photos. Dogs she likes. Because, because. I'm a dog person. And she thinks I'll like them. And I do. But here's the thing. Hypoallergenic dogs. They're out there. You know? I have another friend. She has one. A hypoallergenic dog. Terrible allergies. She has. Really. Really. Bad. But not to her dog. Her hypoallergenic dog. And Yorkies. My Holly. My sweet Yorkie. They're hypoallergenic too. It's a fur thing. Yorkies don't have any. Fur. Like a human. Silky hair. That's what they have. And you know what that means. No fur. No shedding. For a Yorkie. For a hypoallergenic dog. So here's the thing. If scientists can create hypoallergenic dogs. What about us? What about people with pollen allergies? Like me. I mean. We need hypoallergenic pine trees. And azaleas. And weeds. All of that. We need it. We do. Hey. If scientists can mess with our fruit. Fill grocery stores with mutated fruit. Stuff even the raccoons behind my apartment won't eat. Why can't they give us something we actually need? Like hypoallergenic trees, weeds, and bushes. Mutant fruit? Geez. Who needs that? Seriously. These scientists. What are they thinking?"

24. American Cheese

"Dear Elaine," she writes. "About my friend Beth. She thinks I spend too much time with my dog. That I need to get out more. You know. With people. Date more. So she arranged one. A date. With her cousin. A blind date. I know, I know. Could be a disaster. Usually. It is. A disaster. But I said okay. I mean. Beth has a good heart. It was just a lunch date. So I went. Ordered a salad. He got a cheeseburger. And then, and then. I told him I'm vegan. He frowned. Looked at my salad. Told me he only eats burgers. Cheeseburgers. Smothered in melted cheese. American cheese. I said I could relate. He frowned. Again. I mean. I'm vegan. What do I know about cheese? Right? I told him it's for Holly. The cheese. My Yorkie. Holly. It's how I get her to take her vitamin. Half a slice. American cheese. Wrapped around the pill. And it works. It does. Gone. In sixty seconds. The cheese. The pill. Gone. I told him he should try it. He frowned. Again. He thought I was comparing him to a dog. Well. I was. I guess. And then, and then. The cheeseburger was gone. And he was gone. Date over. Poor Beth. She should get a dog. Really. She should. Then she'd know. Why, why, why. A dog is better than a date. A blind date.

And then I'll tell her about the cheese. American cheese. I will. I promise."

25. Dark Night

What does she feel like today? Which postcard? Something light. Bright. A sunflower. Yes. That's it. That's the one. "Dear Elaine," she writes. "This morning. On Tucker Road. Driving to work. I saw a man. Walking. So, so strange. Carrying a black mattress. He was. Draped over his head. And his hands. That's all you could see. Holding the mattress. And his legs. Beneath it. Walking, walking. Just hands and legs. That's it. And black. All of it. The mattress. His clothes. His shoes. Black. Everything. Black. And I wonder, wondered. How can he see where he's going? And yet, and yet. This man. This mattress. So, so black. It reminds me of a book I'm reading. The Dark Night of the Soul. You know. St John of the Cross. Those times in life. So, so dark. When you can't see where you're going. For weeks. Months. The dark night. Miserable. That's what it is. But that's not what I called it years ago. The dark night. No. Marriage. That's what it was. To me. That's what I called it. Marriage. Mine. So, so dark. And yet, and yet. Like this man. On Tucker Road. I kept walking, walking. Searching for light. Some. Any. Until, until. My lawyer. He said it. Divorce. And suddenly. There it was. Light. At last. Can we all sing, Hallelujah? Oh, yeah."

26. Now I've Seen Everything

"Dear Elaine," she writes. "You'll never guess. Never. At the liquor store. King's. One of his stores. The one down the street from my apartment. He's got a new product. Saw the sign this week. On my evening walk. With Holly. Big sign. Right next to the road. Can't miss it. This new product. You'll never guess. Never. Ice cream tacos. Can you believe it? I mean. Whose idea was that? Crazy. Totally. For any store. But a liquor store? Come on. Think about it. No one goes to a liquor store to buy ice cream. No one. And yet, and yet. I can't help wondering. You know. What does it look like? This ice cream taco. So we did it. Me. Holly. We stopped. Tonight. On our evening walk. And went in. We did. We came. We saw. We couldn't believe it. Ice cream tacos. Right there. In the frozen section. Just a big blob of ice cream. Vanilla. Stuffed into a taco shell. Topped with a few sprinkles. And that's it. I mean, seriously. How boring! Crushed. That's what I was. Holly too. So disappointed. Totally. We were. Had to fix that. Had to. Went to the grocery store. Bought a Milk-Bone. For Holly. Her favorite. Bought a pint of Haagen-Dazs Double Belgian Chocolate Chip. For me. You know. Real ice cream. Ate it. All of it. I did. Yeah. We're feeling better now. Much better. Thanks for asking."

27. Sweet Peace

"Dear Elaine," she writes on a new postcard. "Okay. I confess. I struggle with it. Forgiveness. I do. Even though. I know, I know. We're supposed to forgive everyone. To love everyone. We are. For our physical health. Mental health. All of it. I get that. I do. But surely, surely. Not everyone. Right? Not ex-husbands. Not mine. I mean. I can forgive the others. I can. All those who wronged me. Abused me. You know. In the past. Disturbed individuals. That's what they were. Truly. And yet, and yet. Forgive them? I can do that. Yes. Done. But my ex-husband. Disturbed? Oh, yeah. Forgiveness? No way. Not possible. Not for him. Not that I haven't tried. I have. Again and again. Yet I can't. And I don't know why. But then last night. That video I watched. You know. The one on YouTube. About St. Francis. How he loved everyone. Forgave everyone. And yet, and yet. Forgiveness wasn't his focus. Imagine that? Peace. That was his goal. Alrighty! That I can do. Peace. Peaceful. My life. Ever since the day I left him. My ex. Walked away. Me. Gone. Never to return. Sweet peace. This is my life. Now. See? That I can do. Forgiveness? Forget it. Hey. If peace is good enough for Francis. It's good enough for me. Okay, then. I think we're done here. What's next?"

28. Toothpaste

"Dear Elaine," she writes. "Went to PetSmart. Today. Needed more dental treats. You know. For Holly. Her favorite brand. Couldn't find them. Instead, instead. I found this. This. Truly amazing. It is. Are you ready for this? Treats filled with toothpaste. Doggie toothpaste. I kid you not. Crunchy little treats. Full of toothpaste. Pure genius. Isn't it? Two each day. That's all your dog needs. For clean teeth. Healthy gums. Perfect vet exams. Can't get any easier than that. Right? Hey. I'm no fool. Bought two packages. ASAP. You bet I did. But now I'm thinking, thinking. Why not us? Why not dental treats? For humans? Yummy snacks. Filled with edible toothpaste. Like these doggie treats. I mean. Just think. No more flossing. Brushing. Plaque. Tartar. Cavities. Lectures from the hygienist. Torture sessions with the dentist. Fillings. Crowns. Root canals. Imagine that? These dogs. So, so easy. What a life. You know?"

29. All Those Crazies

Daffodils. That's what she wants today. Something light. Cheerful. Nothing dark. No. Not today. She looks through the box. Her collection of postcards. Finds it. A daffodil. That's the postcard. Yeah. That's the one. "Dear Elaine," she writes. "This book I ordered. You know. From Amazon. It came today. Picked it up at the post office. Just now. An exorcist. And the demonic. That's what it's about. Had to order it. Had to. So, so curious. I am. I mean. If you knew my past. My love relationships. Disastrous. Truly. Those bad-news men. Boyfriends. Husband. Crazy, crazy. All of them. Geez. If you knew. You'd understand. But here's the thing. Why me? I'm like a daffodil. Light. Cheerful. And yet, and yet. These crazy men. Demonic. They are. They act like I'm a magnet. Just for them. Insane. That's what it is. And it needs to stop. Their attraction. To me. Stop. Please. I don't want them. Don't like them. Bad-news men. I don't. Maybe this book can help. Maybe, maybe. Who knows? But this I do know. The crazies. Those men. Bad news. They're out there. They are. I mean. A girl can't be too careful these days. You know?"

30. My Authentic Self

"Dear Elaine," she writes. "Should have been a nun. Should have. Would have been a good one too. A good nun. I would have. Instead, instead. I live in the real world. And suffer. It's those blind dates. My girlfriends. Their fault. It is. Well-meaning. They are. But they set me up. All the time. They do. These blind dates. They say, they say. I'll thank them for it. (I won't.) That I need a man in my life. (I don't.) That I'm lonely. (I'm not.) That I need a husband. (I don't.) That single is awful. (It's not.) A blessing. That's what it is. Single. Truly. It is. For me. Like Friday night. My last blind date. Totally freaked. He did. When I showed him my authentic self. You know. The real me. Hey. I couldn't help it. Such a cranky guy. He was. So I called him that. Mr. Cranky. I mean. I was just being honest. Authentic. You know? Big mistake. Grabbed me by the neck. He did. Pulled me through the car window. (I kid you not.) Ended up in the middle of Main Street. On my back. His fingers wrapped around my neck. See? Should have been a nun. Should have. But can't. Not now. Not with Holly. My Yorkie. Sweet Holly. I mean. Who would buy her Milk-Bones? Her favorite treat. No. Can't let Holly down. Can't. Can't be a nun. But I can be authentic. And a dog mom. Both. That I can do. Kinda. Sorta. Well. I'm trying."

31. Punk

She looks through the box on her desk. That's where she keeps them. Her collection of postcards. In that box. But only the pretty ones. Like this one. This postcard. The one she's looking for. A troll doll. That hair. Oh, how she loves it! Shooting up from its head like a fuchsia flame. Just like her old troll doll. The one she used to have. Back in elementary school. The doll she kept in her purse. To slip her hand inside during class. To stroke its hair. So, so silky. That troll doll. That hair. It always made her smile. "Dear Elaine," she writes on this postcard. "Driving home from the grocery store. Holly sitting next to me. Strapped in her car seat. Such a good little girl. My Yorkie. Chewing on a dental bone. Blueberry. Her favorite flavor. But this sign. Tiny. Barely noticeable. On the side of the road. Almost missed it. I did. Punk Flea Market. That's what it said. What? What? What's that? No idea. So I googled it. Huge. It is. This flea market. Here. Today. Right now. In the park. Zillions of vendors. Punk, hippie, rock, counterculture. No. Not my thing. But then, but then. In the vendor photos. That's where I saw them. Troll dolls. Every size and color. Oh, oh, oh! Got to go. Got to! This flea market. I'll take Holly with me. She said she'd go. But only, only. If I give

her a dental bone. Blueberry. Of course. You
know. For the ride. Yeah. That's my girl."

32. Barbie

"Dear Elaine," she writes on a new postcard. "I saw Barbie today. I did. A Barbie doll come to life. This woman. I swear. That's what she looked like. I was out with Holly. You know. Running errands. Took a break and stopped at Starbucks. Got a Mocha Cookie Crumble Frappuccino for me. A Puppuccino for Holly. And there she was. Barbie. No kidding. In a pink convertible. Barbie pink. It was. I swear. Driving down the street. Right in front of us. We were sitting on the patio. You know. Enjoying the sun and our drinks. When she zoomed by. Looked just like my old Barbie doll. I swear. She did. Oh, how I loved that doll! Her long, silky, ash blonde hair. Her bendable legs. Saved my allowance for months. I did. Bought her at Zayre. Spent all my money on her. Every month. No kidding. Lots of outfits. I bought them all. A wardrobe case. Accessories. Everything I could. Except that car. That pink convertible. Too expensive. But everything else? Yeah. I bought it. Only the best for my Barbie. And now, and now. Here she is. Today. Driving past us at Starbucks. In that convertible. Barbie pink. Just think. My Barbie doll come to life. Seriously. Forty years later. What are the odds? You know?"

33. Who Knew?

"Dear Elaine," she writes on a postcard. "It's like this. In this dog magazine. The current issue. Yes. That's the one. This article on dental care. You know. For Holly. For dogs. It says dental chews aren't enough. I mean. They say, they say. They don't do the job. Not completely. Even though my groomer. She's the one. Not me. Never me. No way I'm brushing a dog's teeth. Nope. Not happening. Every month. She does this. Brushes Holly's teeth. My sweet Yorkie. And then, and then. I give her dental chews. Holly, that is. Every day. I do. But these people! These vets. This magazine. They say daily dental chews aren't enough. That I need to do more. Oh, yeah? Like what? Like dental powder. Alright. So I found some. At PetSmart. Kelp. That's what it is. Just sprinkle it on her food. Once a day. That's it. Nutritious to eat. Plus, plus. It dissolves plaque. It does. And tartar. That too. So I bought some. And she likes it. Holly, that is. Okay then. Mission accomplished. Good to have that behind me. What's next?"

34. Dog Mom

She selects another postcard. A Yorkie. Not Holly. But close enough. "Dear Elaine," she writes. "This magazine. The current issue. This dog magazine. There's another article. Fractured teeth. That's what it's about. A major dental problem. It is. Mostly bones. That's the culprit. Chewing on them. But also antlers, cow hooves, yak chews. Seriously? Is this news? I think not. I mean. Really. Come on. Think about it. No way I'd stick something like that in my mouth. Okay. I'm not a dog. But still, but still. Just saying. And there's more. Like this. Like nylon bones. And ice. And tennis balls. Even those. Can you imagine? They all fracture teeth. They do. All of them. All. Or that's what this magazine says. Glad I give Holly dental bones. You know. Those crunchy green things. Look like toothbrushes. They do. In the green package. Yeah. Those. Glad I'm doing something right. Not that I know what I'm doing. I don't. Not a clue. Clueless. That's me. I mean. Holly is my first. You know. Dog. But at least I'm trying, trying. To be a good dog mom. I am. I swear. Trying. Really. I am."

35. Better

The sky? Blue. Has to be blue. That's what she wants. A blue-sky postcard. Okay. Found it. "Dear Elaine," she writes. "So this morning. Pumping gas at Speedway. There I am. The rain is gone. (Can we all sing, Hallelujah?) Nothing but blue skies. The bluest of blue. Truly. And a warm breeze. That too. And bright sunshine. And the scent of fresh-cut grass. (The lawn crew is mowing at Havertys.) And I'm thinking. What a great day to be alive! And I'm thinking. Does it get any better than this? I think not. A few minutes later I'm driving down Tucker Road. And a car pulls into my lane. Right in front of me. And stops. This car. Stops. And turns. Right in front of me. (Crazy people!) I slam on the brakes. My purse flies off the seat. Lands on the floor. And Holly? Still buckled in her car seat. (Thank God!) I look at her. She looks at me. And I say. Puppuccino? She barks. Okay, then. I was wrong. It does get better than this. I mean. There's always a reason. You know? For Starbucks. So there."

About the Author

Laura Stamps loves to create experimental forms for her fiction and poetry. She is the author of over 65 novels, novellas, short story collections, and poetry books, including **It's All About the Ride: Cat Mania** (Alien Buddha Press, 2021), **Dog Dazed** (Kittyfeather Press, 2022), **The Good Dog** (Prolific Pulse Press, 2023), and **Addicted to Dog Magazines** (Impspired, 2023). She is the recipient of a Pulitzer Prize nomination and seven Pushcart Prize nominations. Her short stories, flash fiction, and poetry have been published in over 2000 literary magazines worldwide. You can find her every day on Facebook (Laura Stamps). Or her website: www.LauraStampsFiction.blogspot.com

www.ingramcontent.com/pod-product-compliance
Lightning Source LLC
Chambersburg PA
CBHW070356310726
48977CB00002B/469